batter UP

HALLIE BENNETT

BOOKS BY THIS AUTHOR

CHAPTER ONE

DARCY

Music blares from my smart speaker as I pull the one Eagles shirt I owned out of my closet. Tonight, my roommate and I are going to a baseball game, so I have to show my support for the team even if I don't follow their—schedule that closely. Tugging the tee over my ponytail, I stare at myself in the mirror, trying to decide if I should add a bit of interest. Knotted at the side. Tucked into the front. But every rendition looks bad—cutting me off in weird places, highlighting my round stomach.

A film of tears bubbles up, but I rapidly blink them away—used to the all too familiar refrain. No matter how hard I try, nothing can disguise my fat. Most days it doesn't bother me, and I'm comfortable in my skin even relishing my extra curves. But then something like this removes the blinders to show me that in the end I'm just a chubby woman and no amount of adjusting a tee shirt can hide that fact.

Pulling the cotton hem from the waist of my jeans, I smooth it over my stomach and stare at the box shape I make in the mirror. *Get a grip; it's just a baseball game. It's not like you're going to meet someone.*

Sighing, I flip the light switch off for my room and step into the living room to see if Bethany's ready to go. Standing in the kitchen, she leans against the counter with a bowl of salad in her hands.

"I thought we were eating at the ballpark. Did you forget?" I'd specifically chosen this game because they were holding a special discount on ballpark concessions which I'd mentioned to her the other day.

Bethany's nose wrinkles in disgust as she shakes her head. "No, I'm just not going to eat that junk."

"Oh... I thought we said we were." A sick knot sinks in my stomach at her revulsion. I'd droned on and on about deciding between hot dogs or nachos, trying to get her excited for the full game experience since I knew she wasn't a sports fan when I'd asked her to go with me. Now embarrassment and disgust with myself welled up.

Of course, she wouldn't eat the food. And I should know better, too. Wasn't I just lamenting my weight? Yet here I am about to binge on cheap concessions.

Composing myself, I force a smile. "Let me know when you're ready to go, then. It's okay if we're a little late."

She waves her empty fork as she swallows. "We can leave in a few minutes; I'm almost done."

Nodding, I eye her shorts with the pockets peeking out from the hem and the neon pink crop top. Bethany always dressed for the occasion even for simple walks with just the two of them, reasoning that you never know who you might run into.

At first, I'd tried to keep up, dressing up a little more than usual, so I wouldn't look so out of place next to her. But that actually made me feel worse about myself because my best didn't hold a candle to her natural beauty. Thick raven waves coursed down her back, shiny and sleek, and she kept a toned runner's body. When I'd first moved in, she invited me on her runs, but I refused, not wanting to showcase how out of shape I was compared to her, until she eventually stopped asking.

I tried not to compare myself to her too much, though, because it wasn't her fault she was beautiful, and I wasn't. Plus, she'd earned her fit body while I stayed home reading or watching tv. Didn't mean moments like these didn't hurt, though. Or cause a pang for what was to come in a stadium full of men. Overlooked all the time, I remind myself to prepare for all the flirting we'd encounter at the game— for the men who'd ignore me while hitting on Bethany.

It's not like you're easy to talk to. My shyness prevented me from saying much outside of a brief greeting. Well, shyness and the fear of risking getting to know a man only to have him dismiss me or worse—look at me with pity or disdain.

Bethany tosses her dirty bowl and fork in the sink then turns around with a swish of her ponytail. "Alright, let's do this! Maybe we can snag a hot baseball player," she jokes.

I laugh along, knowing it's not out of the realm of possibilities for her.

Twenty minutes later we pull into the parking garage by the stadium and follow the straggling groups of fans heading inside. The game started thirty minutes ago, but I'm not too concerned. Innings can last forever in baseball, and there's a lot of downtime. I hand Bethany one of the free tickets I'd gotten from work, and it's not long before we find our seats behind the home team's dugout.

"Wow, these are actually really good seats. Your company sprang some serious cash."

"What can I say? Our CEO is a huge fan and probably friends with some executive for the team." I shrug, thankful for our good fortune. One of the many perks my job offered its employees, I thank God that my leap of faith a few months ago had paid off. Stuck in a small town, loneliness and depression defined my days until I'd decided to make a change and moved across the country with nothing but my savings as a safety net. Two weeks later, I'd landed a new job and a shared apartment with Bethany who I'd found through a social media group. Sometimes it still shocked me that I'd made such a bold move—one of the few I'd made in my life.

Bethany and I chat during the first two innings as I explain what's happening, and we try matching the players on the field to the pamphlet with the team roster we'd gotten upon entry. But by the fourth inning, the tantalizing aroma of grilled hot dogs and spicy nachos causes my stomach to growl, announcing its annoyance with being forced to wait an hour later for dinner.

"I'm going to grab some food. Are you sure you don't wanna go with me?"

"I'm good, but I do have to pee. See you in a few!"

We both go our separate ways, and I find the shortest concessions line leading to nachos and a Dr. Pepper—my favorite drink. Juggling the handful, I head over to a condiment stand for a straw and napkins before retracing my steps. Unfortunately, the path back to our seats is fraught with obstacles—vendors, fans, and leashed dogs—and I have to dodge little kids playing tag. A sigh of relief billows up as I near the end of my journey, stepping out to the relative quiet of the outdoor field.

Three guys stand blocking the aisle, waving their beers in the air and talking loudly as I take careful steps down to Aisle J. As I wonder if I can get around them without speaking, one bumps into me and sends my dinner flying all over my front. Ice cold soda drips down my chest to soak the fallen tortilla chips by my feet, and a fierce flush wells under my skin.

I feel like a character on the jumbotron with all eyes on me as a strange silence follows the crash of food. Laughter filters through the buzzing in my head. Apparently, the guys find the accident hilarious.

I can't say I agree.

CHAPTER TWO

CORBIN

S unlight batters my corneas the moment I exit the dugout. "Fuck," I mutter and pull the brim of my cap lower. Evening games are my favorite except for the setting sun part; it never fails to hit at the exact angle to blind a person.

"Hey, boss man! What are you doing down here?" Levins, the Eagles's catcher, calls from the end of the bench where he straps on his pads.

"Thought I'd take in a few innings from the best view in the house."

"Don't you have an entire suite filled with a buffet of food up there?" He points to the owner's box over by the left field foul post. "That looks like a pretty good view to me."

I chuckle and climb up the wooden bench to sit on the concrete shelf behind it. Resting against the cool wall, I say, "True. But sometimes I like to mix things up. Good luck out there, by the way. The Bucks love to steal; they'll keep you busy all night."

Levins stretches his left arm across his chest as he stands up and grins. "I'm counting on it. I love throwing suckers out."

Levins joined the players on the field as they warmed up until the team's called in for introductions and the National

Anthem. Pre-game ceremonies complete, the first inning begins with a raucous cheer from the home team fans.

God, I love this.

Growing up, baseball had never been on my radar. An overweight kid with a penchant for gaming, I spent the majority of my youth indoors behind a screen while my mom worked long hours as a nurse to make up for the deadbeat dad and husband who'd left us when I was eight. Sports didn't matter to me. And if I became envious seeing kids playing together in teams, I comforted myself with the knowledge that I could ask my best friend, Mark, to come over for a game of Super Mario.

Near the end of the second inning, it's still a tied game, and I leave to sit in the stands behind the dugout—not kidding when I said I liked to mix it up. The different points of view of the stadium helps me understand the experience of every fan and fix anything that needs improving like when a few seats were broken up in the nosebleeds a few weeks back. Plus, the energy from the crowd can't penetrate the walls of my ivory tower or rather, my owner's suite.

Winding halls spit me out on the main concourse, and I merge into the rush of people milling about. General chatter floats on the air before converging into feminine voices as I follow two women down Gate 9's tunnel leading to the field. My eyes can't help falling to the one on the right's ass—a round peach perfect for eating or spanking, whichever she preferred.

Seriously, man? Stop being a fucking perv.

Shaking my head, I refocus my attention. It's never a good idea to get distracted by a fan—someone I consider a guest of the stadium which makes me the host. And hosts don't ogle their guests even if the swing of a certain woman's hips does fill his mind with dirty images of fucking her from behind.

Christ!

I swipe a hand over the sweat on my forehead and readjust my cap. Clearly, I've been without a woman too long. *Try all your life.* Running a multi-million-dollar sports organization can do that to you. *Along with being the bullied fat kid for too long before buffing up.* Swallowing hard, I arrive at my aisle, one up and over from the mystery woman, giving me the perfect angle to keep an eye on her—if I want to. Which I don't.

But you could.

The comforting sound of a baseball hitting the catcher's mitt breaks me out of my spiral. Taking a deep breath of the grass-scented air, I settle in for the game, propping my scorebook on a knee and taking notes. After the fourth inning, the curvy brunette leaves with her friend, and I take the opportunity to stand and stretch.

A group of guys in front of me has the same idea as they move to spread out in the center aisle of stairs. Their drunken laughter spikes my annoyance, but when I turn to see what could possibly be so funny, white-hot anger scorches my blood. Covered in a mess of soda and nachos, the mystery woman stood paralyzed; it was obvious one of the men had stumbled into her.

A stillness settles over the scene until a high-pitched "Oink" comes from the dick wearing a Perez jersey, and I see red. Clenching my fist, I contemplate how much trouble I'd get into for knocking out a fan in my stadium. Probably a fine. Possibly a lawsuit.

Worth it.

"Fuck, Kyle, you can't do shit like that after I take a drink." His buddy brandishes a half-empty mug of beer, sloshing pale liquid over the top.

"I couldn't help it; she looks like a fucking pig covered in slop." Turning towards the brunette, Kyle asks. "You know the jumbo size is meant for sharing, right? Though with those rolls, you should probably skip it altogether."

The words slur together but remain clear enough for his friends to bust up in laughter again while the surrounding observers look uncomfortable. Unlocking my phone, I text my head of security a picture and location with instructions to escort the three men off the premises.

As owner of the Eagles, I hold the power to say who can stay in my stadium, and these assholes definitely have to go. Logic wins the day, since I'd rather be taking care of the woman than dealing with cops after punching the guy's face in.

Message sent, I start maneuvering down the aisle to get to her. She glances around the crowd of onlookers—no one was paying attention to the game happening on the field—before bolting up the concrete steps back to the concessions area.

The crack of a bat connecting with the ball draws everyone's attention as cheers rise around me, but I keep my eye on the brunette.

"Hey, wait up!" The words echo in the hall as I hurry forward, placing a staying hand on her shoulder.

She jerks around in surprise, and I hold my hands up in conciliation. "Sorry, I just wanted to get your attention. I saw what those jerks did back there; are you okay?"

Groups of people swerve around us as they walk back to their seats—shooting curious stares at the woman's wet tee.

Though, it's hard to tell if they're drawn by the spectacle or the way her nipples poke at the fabric—hard from the cold moisture.

Her voice draws my gaze back to hers. "I'm fine; thank you. I just need to buy a new shirt and change—not a big deal." She shrugs nonchalantly, but the red coloring her cheeks along with the suspicious gleam of tears in her blue eyes reveals her true feelings.

"Look, I'm Corbin Montgomery." I wait a second to see if recognition dawns, and when it doesn't, I continue but shade the truth. "I know the owner of the team, and he wouldn't want you dealing with this alone. He's already having security ask those guys to leave, so you won't be bothered again."

Her pretty eyes widen in shock behind the big frames of her glasses. "Are you serious? That wasn't necessary...They were drunk and ◇"

"And being dicks. The owner doesn't tolerate the harassment of women or really any of the stadium guests." Which is true. Sometimes things get rowdy at games—especially night games when people tend to let loose after dark. The stadium is known for dealing with problems quickly to keep the environment family-friendly, and this situation was no different.

Except for the fact that I'd like to go down to the parking lot and beat some sense into the offenders. *Forget them. Focus on her. She's the important one.*

The woman still looks concerned, so I take charge and begin ushering her down the tunnel. "Come on, let's get you something dry to wear. We've got plenty of vendors to choose from." Guiding us to the Clubhouse Store by Gate 7, I ask, "So, what's your name?"

"Darcy."

Pretty. Just like her.

CHAPTER THREE

DARCY

I don't know what kind of cruel joke is being played on me to have this hot man help me when I look my absolute worst. I'm sure someone is laughing somewhere, but it's not me. How can I? Cold. Sticky. Humiliated. And he'd probably witnessed it all. Heard what those guys called me.

Pig.

God, the word echoes in my head and heart. How many times can I almost cry tonight? Because the tell-tale symptoms warned of the coming tide, and I'm not sure I have the strength to ward them off again.

"Here we are. Take whatever you want; it's on the house." My brows raise; Corbin must be really close with the owner if he wields the power to offer me free merchandise. Reeling in my emotions, I attempt to concentrate on the problem at hand and scan the racks with him trailing close behind. A clean, fresh scent envelops me, and I know it's him. The store is empty except for us and the attendant which makes me feel a little better; more witnesses to my ordeal would be the icing on an already sucky cake.

"Do you have a favorite player? We can get you a jersey, if you want," he offers as he flicks through a couple of hangers. I appreciate the gesture, but I'm not going to take advantage of his friend's kindness by springing for one of the most expensive items. Red and white jerseys hang from the wall in a specially designated spot away from the regular shirts and hoodies delineating their higher value.

"Honestly, I don't really follow the team. My tickets were a gift from my job."

"Oh? Where do you work?" He stops and takes his cap off, slapping it lightly against his thigh in a nervous gesture, a cute blush blooming. "Wait, sorry. That sounded creepy like I can find you at your office. I meant to ask what do you do?"

I smile briefly at his awkwardness, making me forget my own insecurities at the moment. It puts me a bit at ease to be reminded that he's human even if he is attractive as sin with dark auburn waves laying flat on his head before he runs a hand through it while brown eyes study my reaction.

"I work in research. Dealing with numbers mostly."

"Sounds fun," he teases and pulls a red tee off the rack. "How about this one?"

My smile fades as I look at the shirt. It's a woman's size, a large, but I know it'll be way too small for me. All at once the reality of what we're doing hits me. This isn't some social call where a man's flirting with me; we're searching for a replacement tee after I got called a fat pig.

Nothing you haven't called yourself before.

The dark taunt slithers through my mind.

Reaching blindly for the nearest shirt towards the back of a rack, I snag a 5X men's size. At least it'll be guaranteed to fit. "This will do. And I can pay for it; it's fine."

Corbin's head tilts to the side as he looks between me and the shirt, confusion clear on his handsome face, but he just says,

"Like I said, it's covered. You just go change; a dressing room is over there." He motions to a small door to the side, and I scurry over. Five minutes later I'm draped in stiff cotton with my ruined shirt folded in my hands.

A giant eagle emblazons the front while a list of the team roster fills the back. The hem almost meets my knees, but I'm covered even if I look terrible. A flash of all the movies I've seen where the woman comes out in her boyfriend's tee looking sexy and how much the man loves it crosses my mind. If this was Corbin's tee, it'd be clinging to me in all the wrong places. No sexy image there.

As if he'd date you in the first place. You think he wants a woman other men laugh at?

Knowing the truth, I rub a hand over my heart and meet Corbin's friendly gaze. "Feeling better?" He holds out a plastic bag for me to drop my old shirt in before we walk out.

"Much. Thank you again," I say, gripping the bag tightly. "Oh, and thank your friend, too. It was really nice of him to step in; I feel like this kind of stuff is way below his paygrade." An anxious laugh bubbles up—not liking being the cause of trouble even if I technically didn't start it.

"He likes keeping a finger on the pulse of the stadium. Things like this definitely fall under that category. Now, since your meal was ruined, how about I treat you to dinner?"

A pity meal giving him more time to wake up and wonder what the hell he's doing with her? No, thank you.

"I can't. My friend's probably wondering where I am." After saying it, I realize I'd forgotten about Bethany. A fact I feel terrible about when it occurs to me that she's most likely sitting alone with no clue as to what's happening with the game or where her roommate went. If that happened to me, I'd start to panic.

"I thought of that." He looks up from his phone where he's rapidly typing something. "Damn, that sounded weird, too. I swear I'm not a stalker or serial killer or whatever. I just remembered seeing you with someone. A member of the staff is notifying her of your situation; she'll be fine."

Another round of shock sweeps through me at the brazen move. I stop walking and move to the side of the walkway for others to pass. "I can't just leave her alone; that's rude. And while I appreciate the generosity, it's unnecessary. This all feels like it's been blown way out of proportion and ⬦"

A wave of emotion stalls the words in my throat, and breathing suddenly becomes a chore. Bringing a hand to my neck, I try to choke out another sentence, but the only thing that falls are tears as I reach my limit for the day. Mortified by the swift attack, I brush a hand over my cheeks and apologize. "I'm sorry....I... I don't know why..."

Corbin brings an arm around my shoulders, and we start moving again, though I can't see where we're going through the sheen of tears covering my eyes. "Shh...you're going to be alright. I've got you. Come on; we're going to go somewhere private."

He pulls a badge out of his pocket and hovers it over a metal plate next to an elevator causing the doors to open. *Really good friends with the owner.* Dashing inside, he hits a button, and they start going up. A few minutes later, he opens another door—this one leading to a suite filled with leather couches and a stainless-steel buffet laid out on one wall.

Who is this man?

CHAPTER FOUR

CORBIN

I breathe a sigh of relief upon seeing everything I'd asked for set up when we enter my suite. It occurred to me when Darcy was changing that I could wrangle more time with her by providing a replacement dinner, so I'd messaged one of the staff to bring up some food from Tres Amigos, a popular Mexican restaurant in the stadium.

Though dinner was the last thing on my mind now as Darcy cried in my arms. The onslaught of emotions is no surprise after what she's been through but seeing her distress tears me up inside.

Closing the door behind us, I pull her into a hug. "Baby, I'm so sorry. Forget what those assholes said; it's not true." She shudders, her cheek resting against my chest and setting her glasses askew. "Please, sweetheart, stop crying..."

Somehow my whispered words transform into soft kisses as I ache to take away her pain. I'm not sure what's come over me—this urge to possess and protect her riding me hard despite us being strangers. My hand tilts her head up as my mouth dips lower and lower until our lips meet.

Like a deer in headlights, she freezes. Warnings sound in my head that I should stop, that I'm taking advantage. But I can't pull away. No matter how loud my mind's shouting at me, there's a stronger draw urging me to comfort her anyway I can even if it's just my mouth loving hers.

Love? Too soon, man.

But the idea doesn't scare me as much as it should.

Cupping her cheek, I brush a thumb over her bottom lip, tracing the inner softness with my tongue until she opens for me fully—a sweet little whimper coming from her throat. A sound that forces my hard-on against the zipper of my jeans, eager to please her.

"Don't worry, baby. I've got you." My tongue sweeps along hers—shy in the wake of my invasion—but I keep coaxing until she tentatively follows my lead. *So, this is what everyone's talking about.*

I've kissed a few women in the past, but it never felt like it should or how the movies, books, or music described it. Which is probably why I'm still a virgin at thirty-two. The lackluster kisses coupled with a long-held insecurity about my body made the thought of sleeping with any of the women about as appealing as having a batting average of zero.

My imagination kept my hand busy, but now I envisioned Darcy starring in those dreams. I want to experience everything with her which sounds insane, but what the hell? I'm a virgin in his thirties; I've had enough time to take the slower route, building a relationship.

I want Darcy, and I want her now. Fuck the consequences.

Tightening my arm around her waist, I back her into the wooden door and press deeper into her body. Warm curves mold to my firm body, and I can't resist thrusting my cock between her thighs and rubbing hard, wanting to get us both off.

"Corbin...Wait." Darcy twists her head to the side and pushes at my shoulders. "You don't have to do this. We *shouldn't* be doing this. We're strangers."

Nipping at her ear, I disagree. "I want to do this, and a hell of a lot more. Fuck that strangers shit." I lick down her neck as her hands tangle in my hair in a move I hope means surrender until her stomach growls. *Fuck*. Some caretaker I am. Can't even feed my woman before needing to fuck her against any available service.

My woman?

"Damn, I'm sorry, baby. I got sidetracked and forgot you hadn't eaten." Wiping away the last of her tears, I step back, grab her hand, and lead us to the food set up.

"What's all this?" Darcy asks and lifts the lids off a couple of pans.

"Tres Amigos. If you don't care for Mexican, I can have something else sent up."

"You weren't kidding about knowing the owner. How'd he even manage this?" Guilt kicks me in the gut at my deception. Women tended to treat me differently once they knew I made more in a fiscal year than your average Joe, so I appreciated pretending to be just another fan at the park. But I didn't like lying to Darcy, especially not after our kiss.

"It only took a couple of texts." I lift my shoulders casually and stuff my hands in my pockets. "And it's actually me; I own the Eagles. I just don't like leading with that title because people can act funny after they know. Sorry for lying."

Darcy replaces the lid on a tray full of chicken, avoiding my gaze, before walking over to the small kitchenette. "Oh, um...no problem. It makes sense to keep it a secret at first." Wetting a paper towel, she starts scrubbing at her arms which must be sticky from the accident. *Something else you forgot.* Unfortunately, the sleeves of the oversized tee reached her elbows, forcing her to keep shoving them up to get out of her way.

When she'd first emerged swimming in the tee, an image of her naked underneath standing in my bedroom sent arousal rocketing straight to my cock. But then a wash of empathy followed because I understood the need to cover up, to hide yourself out of fear—I'd done it enough times as a kid. It didn't help that those assholes insulted her body, too.

"Here, let me help." I step closer, but she jerks back, dripping water to the hardwood floor.

"Sorry." Another blush pinkens her cheeks and her eyes dart to the door. "I really should go. I don't know what came over me earlier, but I'm fine now. Really. And the kiss..." She pauses, keeping her eyes on her grey converse shoes. "I appreciate your kindness. I'll let you get back to the game now. Who knows how much I've already caused you to miss?"

I couldn't care less about the game. There'd be another one tomorrow and the day after that. One hundred and six more to be exact. What mattered was this moment with Darcy.

"Fuck the game. I'm right where I want to be. And you can't tell me you're not starving." I glance down at her stomach, remembering its earlier disgruntlement.

Blue eyes dart between me, the door, and the food before finally settling on the buffet. *Thank God hunger won.* Though I wish a different type had won out, and she'd chosen me. But I'll take what I can get.

The night lights flicked on outside warning me of the limited time we have before the game ends.

I need to make it count.

CHAPTER FIVE

DARCY

What the hell am I doing?

I sit across from Corbin at a table in front of a large window that overlooks the field. The players are so far away I can barely make out their names on the back of their jerseys or see the ball which makes it difficult to follow the game.

Not that it would be possible anyway while having dinner with Corbin, quite possibly the most attractive man I've ever seen. Or at least the only man to get me all hot and bothered.

Although my shyness and fear of rejection kept me from interacting with most men, a part of me also feared how I'd respond if I even managed to snag a guy's interest. I've kept myself distant for so long, and my imagination's built up a dream guy impossible to attain. What if I wasn't physically attracted to the kind of guy that wanted me?

Not a problem with Corbin. No, his kiss had set me ablaze even as doubts tried to push to the forefront. My mind couldn't figure out his intentions. Why was he being so nice to me? Kissing me?

Surely, this goes beyond a baseball team owner's job description. Which brought up another concern. A rich, handsome, single man wanted me? Darcy Evans? Twenty-nine-year-old virgin with curves to spare?

The math didn't make sense. And I should know; research and numbers made up the majority of my days.

"Is something wrong? Like I said, I can have something else brought up," Corbin says, eyeing my untouched plate.

"No, this is fine; thank you." I take a bite of the chicken fajita I'd made. He'd ordered way too much food for just the two of us, and even if I'd decided to eat normally, I wouldn't have made a dent. As it stood, I limited my portion to a handful of tortilla chips with guacamole and salsa along with two fajitas on the small round tortillas.

He didn't seem like the men who'd called me names, but I wasn't about to prove them right in front of Corbin by stuffing my face.

As if reading my mind, he asks, "Are you sure you have enough? No need to be shy. I like a woman who can eat." He flashes a teasing grin, and I smile weakly back.

He says it like it's true. But doubt cuts through me. Lowering one hand, I tug at the tee around my stomach, making sure it's not conforming to the roundness, before taking another bite of dinner and shaking my head. "I'm good; thanks."

"You don't have to keep thanking me, you know. I'm happy to feed you...and clothe you, too, I guess." A short laugh comes from him. "But that last part doesn't sound right."

I return a genuine smile this time. "Yeah, not really. But I appreciate the sentiment. I just want you to know that I'm grateful for all you've done for me tonight."

Like a knight in shining armor, he swept in and carried me off to safety. Too bad I'm the pumpkin—not Cinderella—and my time's almost up. Corbin may be kind tonight; he may want to kiss the damsel he saved.

But come tomorrow, I'll be forgotten.

Hell, if he walked me back to my seat and saw Bethany, I'd be history before they even said, "Hello".

"I'm just glad I was there. I like to sit in different spots of the stadium to stay on top of the inner workings. Any other night and I would've missed you." He frowns as if the realization doesn't sit well. *Or it's the Mexican food he's downing like he hasn't had a meal in ages.*

"Luck was with us, I suppose."

"Or fate."

"Aren't they one and the same?" I take a sip of water, curious about his answer.

"Not necessarily. Luck is good things happening to you, but fate says they were meant to." Warm brown eyes search mine after the explanation, but I'm at a loss for words. He can't be saying what I think he's saying...Right?

That somehow we're meant to be?

My gaze traces the strong line of his shadowed jaw down over his broad shoulders, and I can't imagine this man could be meant for me. It would never work.

I'd be uncomfortable all the time, feeling guilty for reading instead of working out with him—something I already felt with Bethany. They'd be perfect together. Beautiful, healthy and going on all the cute couples adventures I see on Instagram.

"That's a lot of credit to give the universe or whatever. But I don't think I believe in all of that," I say before finishing my last chip on my plate. Checking my phone, I see multiple messages from Bethany and the scoreboard across the field shows we're in the top of the ninth leading the opposing team by three. "Looks like it's time for me to go; the game's almost over. And thank you for the meal. It was delicious."

I worry he's going to come up with another excuse for me to stay, but he tosses his napkin down and nods. Disappointment curls around my heart. *Oh, please...What did you expect? Him to lock you away with him?*

The idea sent a shiver of anticipation straight to my core, and I made a note to lay off the dark romance novels for a bit. Because I should not be getting turned on by the thought of a man holding me against my will.

It doesn't take long to get back to my seat, and I gird myself for Corbin's reaction when he sees Bethany.

"There you are! Some staff member told me what happened. Are you okay?" Bethany jumps from her seat to hug me before her eyes drift over to Corbin, and she flashes him a flirty smile.

"Hi, I'm Bethany. I take it you're the guy that helped our poor Darcy?" I wince at the description and stand awkwardly between them. The aisle is narrow, not meant to accommodate people standing and chatting, but Bethany doesn't seem to care.

Corbin dips his head in assent and asks, "Before I leave, can I get your number and maybe your last name?"

"Pretty bold of you considering we just met, but I like a man who knows what he wants. It's 910 ◈"

"I meant Darcy." Corbin's gaze bores into mine, and I feel like I'm on display again as the people seated in front of us turn to see what's happening. Perplexed by his request and eager to get out of here, I rattle off my number.

"Thanks; I'll call you later." And with those parting words, he jogs back up the stairs and out of my life despite his promise.

"Okay, so when he calls, tell him that I'm out for a run with my friend, Chris, but I'll return his call when I'm free," Bethany says as we take our seats.

My brows knit in confusion. Didn't she hear me give him *my* number? "Why would he ask about you?" The question feels rude, but I'm not understanding her train of thought here.

Bethany's head tilts as she raises a hand to explain as if I'm a five-year-old. "He's playing hard to get. Ignoring me and asking for my friend's number in an attempt to pique my interest. Then he'll hit you up for more information, and that's when you'll let him know that I can play the game, too." She smirks as if any of that makes sense to me.

But I suppose she would know better, since she regularly goes on dates with men while I stay at home reading about fictional ones. Maybe she has a point. I figured once Corbin met Bethany it would be game over for me anyway. The fact that she thinks he'll call when I don't probably means she's right.

"Sounds fun," I mutter, watching as the last batter is thrown out at first base. *Finally*. "I'll let you know what he says."

Then cry about giving my first kiss to a man who wants my roommate.

CHAPTER SIX

CORBIN

That night I scroll the internet searching for Darcy's social media profiles, hoping for more insight into my mystery woman. Unfortunately, her profiles are set to private which prevents a stalker like me from discovering much of anything.

I sigh and toss the phone to the nightstand by my bed. Tomorrow couldn't come soon enough, though a piece of me worried that she wouldn't answer when I called. She'd seemed flustered when I asked—not to mention her friend butting in. That had really annoyed me.

Turning off the lamp, I try to fall asleep but thoughts of Darcy swirl in my mind, taunting me, until finally I reach down my sweatpants and take hold of my erection—a familiar move. My eyes close, seeing Darcy in that oversized Eagles tee—except this time she's naked underneath like I wanted.

In my mind, she's fresh from a shower, cotton clinging to her wet skin. I slowly walk closer until I lean into her with a hand braced on the wall above her head. My grip tightens as I imagine Darcy's hand replacing mine, jerking me off in slow strokes before gradually increasing. Soon I'm hoping I can enjoy the real thing with Darcy, but for tonight, my hand will have to do.

THE PHONE RINGS AS I sit in my office, praying that Darcy answers my call, but after a few more rings, it goes to voicemail. Okay, not a problem. She probably doesn't answer numbers she doesn't recognize which is smart.

"Hey, Darcy! It's Corbin from the stadium last night. I wanted to know if you're free for lunch tomorrow? Or the day after that? Whatever works for you is good. Just give me a call ◈" The message cuts off with a beep, and I curse my stupid babbling. It's obvious I don't have much experience asking women out because I have no game.

Which isn't that big of a surprise considering women don't really care—they hear that I own a baseball team and dollar signs cha-ching over their heads. No need for me to even try. Setting the phone face up on my desk, I try to focus on work instead of obsessing over hearing from Darcy.

As if she heard my plea, the buzzing of a call coming in goes off, and I snatch up the phone and swipe to answer. "Darcy." Her name sounds like the answer to a prayer. *Tone it down.* "I mean, hey! Thanks for calling me back." *Smooth.*

"Hi..." She sounds hesitant. Like she's wondering why the fuck she's talking to me. "Was there something you forgot last night? You don't have to go through the trouble of lunch; you can tell me now."

My brow wrinkles in confusion. I'm not sure what she's talking about. "No, nothing like that. I just want to have lunch with you."

"Is this about Bethany?"

And now I'm really confused. "Your friend?" A small laugh leaves me. "No, it's not about her. It's about you." *And the fact that I want you to sit on my face.* But I can't say that or risk her blocking me from ever contacting her again.

"Oh." Silence hangs in the air.

Deciding to take charge, I say, "So, tomorrow at one? We can meet here at the stadium." It might be unconventional bringing a date to work, but I want to be alone with Darcy—not in a restaurant full of people. Besides, it could be fun showing her around what I've worked hard to build.

When I bought the team a few years ago, it'd be a struggling franchise with a decaying stadium and players past their golden years. Primed for an influx of new blood and cash.

"Sure, I'll see you then." We hang up, and I sigh a breath of relief. One obstacle down.

CHAPTER SEVEN

DARCY

My heart's beating out of my chest as I cross the street to where I see Corbin standing and waving. Bethany's words run through my mind on replay. *He's using you to get to me. It's all a game.* But why didn't he mention her on the phone?

Why have me come here for lunch?

"Hey, you made it!" His bright smile disarms me and sends butterflies fluttering in my stomach. I hope I don't make a fool of myself today by clamming up with nerves.

"It's a lot easier to navigate around here without a game going on." I joke, grateful for the ability to form some kind of normal sentence. But it is true. Though I enjoy a night out at the ballpark, I hate driving around downtown and figuring out where to park in a sea of cars and people.

"Next game, I'll get you a special pass, so you won't have to worry about any of that," Corbin says as he guides me through the empty stadium—only a few maintenance workers line the halls—a stark contrast to game night.

"Oh, you don't have to do that. I actually get a free parking pass with the tickets from work."

"This is better. We have special parking for players and team personnel along with their families or significant others."

"But I'm none of those things." I point out.

He doesn't respond, instead we reach our destination where more food is set out. It feels like deja vu again, and a debilitating thought that all he thinks I want to do is eat forms.

AFTER WE FINISH EATING, he takes me on a tour of the stadium which is actually pretty cool.

"It's a lot quieter here than normal because the team's out of town for a stretch of away games." Corbin explains as we walk out onto the empty field. It's surreal standing on the grass that professional baseball players stand on—grass that I've seen on tv all my life but haven't had the opportunity to experience up close. I can't believe that I am here right now because some drunk guys doused me with my food last night. We round the bases, and I stare up in awe at the rows of seats surrounding us.

"This is so amazing; I can't believe you own all of this. Aren't you a little young?"

Corbin laughs. "You're not the first one to make that comment. I actually started out in the tech world, and I sold an app a few years ago which is where I got the money to buy the team. Although by MLB standards it was actually a pretty good bargain. The team was kind of flailing, and they needed a revitalization. So, it worked out for both of us."

"What made you want to buy a baseball team? Did you use to play? Are you some famous baseball player I've never heard of?"

Corbin smiles. "No, not quite. I actually didn't play baseball until later. I wasn't one of the Little League kids or anything. I was home a lot by myself while my mom worked. It wasn't until she met my stepdad that I got into the game. He was a baseball coach, so the summer after my sophomore year she had me join his team. That's when I learned to love baseball. Plus, I was a chubby kid, and it got me in shape. I got a scholarship to play in college, nothing fancy or anything—a D2 School—but it was something considering we didn't have a lot of money."

I'm surprised to hear that he didn't grow up rich. I assumed men who own professional sports team come from a long line of families that own sports teams or racehorses or yachts—whatever rich people can use to play with since they don't need to work. But hearing his story of how he fell in love with baseball and apparently didn't always look like an Adonis endeared him to me even more.

He didn't act like any millionaire guy or at least what I would expect a guy like that to act. He was down-to-earth and could even be awkward sometimes. I remembered his blush from yesterday, his babbling on the phone, and his voicemail. It sets me at ease. Maybe I can handle being in a relationship or something with this guy.

Though I still don't totally know what he expects from me. As if on cue, Corbin turns to me as we open a gate leading from the field to the stadium seats and walk up the stats between the aisles.

Corbin asks, "So, now that you've seen the lowest part of the stadium, do you want to check out the view from the nosebleeds?" He points up to the very top rows. I follow his direction and nod.

"Let's do it."

It doesn't take us long to get an elevator, and we find ourselves at the top row looking down the field. The view of the city is spectacular, and I'm kind of jealous that he gets to see this whenever he wants.

"So, are you enjoying today?" Corbin asks.

"Yeah, of course. This is a once-in-a-lifetime experience," I say.

"It doesn't have to be," he says, kind of shy but staring deeply into my eyes.

My nose scrunches. "What do you mean?"

He runs a hand through his hair and shakes his head. "Isn't it obvious? I really like you, Darcy."

Now, I'm really shocked. "Why? Really, why? I mean that sounds terrible, but I don't understand. You could have anyone. My roommate, Bethany, really likes you."

His eyes narrow. "I don't give a damn about your roommate; I care about what you think." My eyes widen and those butterflies from earlier start up again.

How do I respond? I don't think he's lying but a part of me feels like it's a trick. Like he's going to turn around and make fun of me for actually believing he'd be interested in me. I know he's not that type of guy or at least he doesn't seem like it based on today, but what do I really know about him?

"You don't believe me, do you?" he asks.

"I'm trying, I really am, but this isn't normal for me. These things happen to Bethany or one of my other friends."

"Well, I can't speak for any of those people who chose your friends over you except that they're idiots, and I think God for that because it means that I have a shot. Right?" The vulnerable question melts me even more. "You know, I can talk this to death, but I feel like actions speak louder than words for you..." he trails off, and I wonder what he means. What kind of action?

He steps closer to brush a hand down my cheek. "Something like this."

His mouth lowers to mine, the slight shadow on his jaw scratching against my cheek. This is my first kiss, and I don't know how romantic it is in an empty baseball. But it feels pretty magical to me. My mouth opens to welcome him, and I try my best to mimic his moves, since I don't know what I'm doing. All I've learned about kissing is from books and movies which means I haven't learned much at all.

But Corbin doesn't seem to notice; he groans and an arm wraps around my waist, pulling me closer. For the first time, I feel a man's erection, and it makes me wet thinking of rubbing against it.

You hardly know the man; calm down.

CHAPTER EIGHT

CORBIN

S he tastes like a cherry popsicle on a hot summer day.
My favorite.

I wasn't sure how she'd respond to my kiss, but we weren't getting anywhere by talking. Darcy was skittish; I want to prove that I'm worth trusting. That she's all I want.

Clearly, her past hasn't been the great with men—used to being overlooked. I understood the feeling all too well, even if it'd been years since I'd encountered it. Something like that lingered—the memory of being chosen last. *Or never.*

Growing up awkward and overweight in school had burned the feeling deep into my bones. But I don't want to hang onto it anymore or let Darcy do the same. Maybe together we can overcome it.

Her tongue shyly brushes against mine, and the blood pounds in my chest. Running a hand down her back, I cup her ass and urge her forward against my hard-on, the truth of my need for her on full display. Her breath catches at the action, but her nails dig into my shoulders for purchase as her body works against mine. The slight pain serves as proof that she wants me, too.

I wonder if we can get each other off just like this; the thrill of finding out shoots down my spine. And a fantasy I've imagined when my mind drifted during games flashes in my mind. Breaking away, I trail kisses up her cheek to her ear where soft curls tickle my nose. "I've had a certain fantasy about being up here alone with a woman. Want to help me act it out?"

"What is it?" Her husky voice is sexy as hell. I can't wait to hear it calling my name as she comes, and my attention drops to her slightly swollen mouth. That'll be another fantasy to check off.

"I want to eat your pussy all the way up here while you look out over the city." The crude request races out of my mouth before she has a chance to stop it. It's fast—we've known each other for less that twenty-four hours—but I'm so hungry for her. And after all, I said actions speak louder than words, right?

Hard to argue that I don't desire her when my tongue's buried in her pussy.

"You want to..." She stops, eyes wide—flustered with red heat staining her cheeks. "Now? What if someone sees?"

Relief wells up that it's not an immediate negative answer. "You know how high we are? One hundred and thirty-five feet. And no one's around; it's practically a ghost town here during away games."

She glances around as if a spy is going to pop out to catch us in the act, but it's empty. We're little blips up here. It's hard enough making out the game from this height. Someone discovering me on my knees for her? Practically impossible.

"It's up to you, but I really want you to say yes." I step back, giving her room to think, while my gaze travels over her curves. Maybe if she lets me eat her out now, later she'll let me fuck her against my desk.

Hell, let the woman breathe before you become a sex maniac. But I'm tired of being a virgin; I want to cash in my v-card.

Today.

With Darcy.

"I may regret this, but..." I hold my breath as she pauses and takes a deep breath before releasing it with a shrug. "Yes."

The biggest, dumbest grin breaks out on my face at her acquiescence. My girl just agreed let me go down on her—in public, outside in my stadium—exactly like I dreamed.

"So, how should we do this? These aisles and seats aren't that big..." She looks doubtfully at the layout, but I'll make it work. In my imagination, she's sitting in a seat, but I'll take her riding my face as I lay beneath her on the concrete. I'm not picky.

"Sit here." I gently guide her down to Seat J. *About to become my favorite place in the whole stadium.* Once she's seated, I kneel before her. It's tight, but we fit. My back grazes the back of the plastic seat behind me, but that won't be a problem for long. Not when I lean forward to help Darcy get into a comfortable position.

My hands drift up her bare legs to slide under her dress. "Let's remove these." Warm heat meets my palms, and she lifts up, so I can pull her panties down, stuffing them in my back pocket. "And prop your leg over this arm. Same with the other."

"Are you sure about this?" I hear the doubt creeping into her voice at being so exposed and know I'm running out of time before she backs out of the whole thing.

Placing a calming hand on her thigh, I brush a light kiss over the inside of her knee. "We can stop whenever you want to, but I guarantee that no one can see us. And I'm going to make it worth your while."

I hope.

I haven't actually done this before, but I figure I'll learn as I go. It's just like kissing, right? Just lower—the sweet, sensitive center kept hidden. Her body should tell me if I'm doing it right, I think. God, I hope I don't fuck this up.

CHAPTER NINE

DARCY

Nerves and arousal swirl inside clouding my judgement—otherwise would I really be sitting here with my legs spread, waiting for a near-stranger to put his mouth on me? Doesn't seem like a rational decision, yet here I am.

He waits for my consent, his bearded cheek resting against my knee, dark brown eyes understanding yet fiery with need. "Go ahead; I trust you."

A massive statement coming from me, but it doesn't feel like a lie. No matter how quickly we've come together or my personal doubts about my weight and attractiveness, Corbin doesn't have any qualms. And it's unfair to keep believing the worst will happen when maybe it won't—especially as we continue down this path.

The corners of Corbin's mouth quirk up in an adorable grin before he marks a path to my center with gentle kisses. I've dreamed of this moment for a long time; it's always featured highly in my fantasies and books I read. To now get to experience it? I pray it doesn't fall short of my expectations.

Way to be positive.

When his hot breath coasts over my exposed flesh, I shiver and close my eyes. I know he said something about looking out over the city as he did this, but screw that. This is my focus—him and me.

One long lick works its way up to my clit before Corbin's lips wrap around the sensitive bundle of nerves and lightly sucks. My hands clench his shoulders for purchase as I buck up into his mouth, a breathy gasp renting the air.

"Corbin..." His tongue dips inside me in shallow thrusts before circling my opening and moving back to my clit. Rough fingers replace the absence and perform a come-hither motion eliciting a low moan from my throat.

"Mmm...Do that again, baby. I want to hear you." Corbin repeats the move, and like a good girl, I give in to his request—another sound of pleasure rising up. Our eyes meet as he continues stroking, and the intimacy of the moment steals my breath. More than the physical intimacy alone. Desire and a tenderness shine from Corbin's gaze, and that same care emanates from his body, in his touch.

I lift a trembling hand and brush the back of it against his cheek. A low hum vibrates from him as he nuzzles my palm. "Darcy... Tell me you feel this, too. That it's not just me with this overpowering need."

A vulnerability steals over his expression. Again, I'm struck by the contrast from his usual confident demeanor, but I suppose we all deal with insecurities.

"I don't understand what's happening, but it's not just you." The soft admission comes quickly, hoping to ease his worry. I should feel strange having such an intense exchange while my thighs are still spread for him, but gratitude courses through me, instead. This is my first time with a man, and I'd always pictured giving myself to someone I loved—not a stranger.

Yet, Corbin broke through those defenses with hardly a fight from me with his willingness to be vulnerable and checking on me constantly to make sure I was with him the entire time. A shudder passes through Corbin before a smile breaks out and leans up for a quick, hard kiss.

I taste myself on his lips, and the illicit flavor shocks me. "I suppose I should finish what I started? You liked it?" His husky voice reignites my desire as I nod in affirmation.

"Yes...very much."

Lowering his head, Corbin increases the speed of his thrusts as he alternates between gentle and hard sucks that soon have me grasping his wavy hair in a tight grip and arching into his mouth. The tension building in my body releases in a wave of pleasure more intense than any orgasm I've given myself.

Corbin continues licking and stroking until the waves subside, and a dreamy haze of satisfaction settles over me. Swallowing hard, my blood pounds in my ears as the slight buzz travels down my body.

Corbin tenderly moves my feet back to the concrete and sits next to me, wrapping an arm over my shoulders. "How do you feel?"

"Perfect," I say with a smile, and then I tease. "And hot. The sun is shining right on top of us; let's hope we haven't gotten sunburned."

Looking up, he shades his eyes with a hand before shooting a worried glance my way. "You're right. I didn't think of that." He ushered us to their feet, and fifteen minutes later we stood in his air-conditioned office. Our interlude in the nosebleeds is becoming more and more unbelievable.

I let Corbin go down on me in public.

And I want him to do more now.

CHAPTER TEN

CORBIN

I'm not sure how she's going to react now that we're in my office—back to reality. I don't want to push her, but after the taste I've had, I need more.

"How are you feeling? Okay?" I ask, trying to gauge where her head's at as she roams around my office studying the frames of articles about important games and pictures with baseball legends.

"Strangely enough, yes." A small laugh bubbles up, and she smiles at me which sends a rush of relief through my bones. *Thank God.* "Although..."

My premature celebration skids to a halt as she trails off. *Although...what?*

It was nice, but it's a one-time thing?

She didn't enjoy it as much as I thought she did?

Turning to face me, her hands play with a stray string on her dress while her gaze fixates on the outfield behind me. "I don't understand why it happened. I mean I understand *why*." She chuckles nervously. "But not why you chose me? Geez, that sounds bad...You're attractive, fit, and I barely ◈"

I cut her off as my hands engulf hers to stop the fidgeting. "You're sexy as hell, curves and all. You know I used to look a lot different before baseball. Kids bullied me so much for my weight

47

that eventually I took to hiding out in my room and playing on my computer."

I've never shared that part of my story with anyone. Most people know me as I am now, never suspecting that I grew up poor and chubby. But I want Darcy to know all of me—my past, present, and hopefully, be part of my future.

"What? I'm so sorry," she says, the gentle sympathy in her blue eyes soothing that young boy I'd been.

"So, you see, I understand not feeling good enough or worrying about your looks. But I'm telling you, I don't care. I think you're beautiful inside and out."

"You barely know me to say such a thing," she counters.

"I know enough. What do people say? When you know you know?"

"That's about love. We're not in love." Her voice gets quiet as she meets my knowing gaze. It's wild and fast, but I know she's mine—the one meant for me. And I've felt it from the moment I saw her last night.

"I don't expect you to say anything yet, but I don't want anyone else. You're it for me; I'm in this for the long haul, baby." I lay my cards on the table, waiting for her response. While a similar declaration would be nice, I'd settle for her continuing to see me. Hopefully, this day and conversation hasn't scared her off for good.

She licks her lips, and my eyes narrow on the action, remembering how she tasted. If Darcy would let me, I'd make her so happy, give her so much pleasure, she'd never want for anything.

"Take me home."

My heart plummets. Not what I expected. Letting go of her, I step back and circle my desk—the physical barrier mirroring the emotional one he feared she was erecting between them.

"If that's what you want, I understand. I'll walk you out if that's okay."

"I meant take me to *your* home." Darcy takes a deep breath then shyly continues. "As romantic as this stadium is, I'd prefer more privacy, and Bethany's at my apartment."

A hesitant grin tugs at my mouth as I work out what she means. "You want to go home. With me. You're not running for the hills because I just told you that I'm falling hard and fast for you?"

"Maybe that's what I should do, but it's not what I want. Something must be in the water because I feel this strange connection, too." Her shoulders rise in a confused shrug, but I'll take it. Anything to spend more time with Darcy.

"Your car or mine?" I ask.

"I'll follow you in mine." She offers the compromise, and I nod in agreement.

"Sounds good. Let's get going." I pull my car keys from my pocket, eager to leave now that it's decided.

CHAPTER ELEVEN

DARCY

Twenty minutes later, we enter a gated community, and I park next to Corbin in front of a two-story brick home. The pretty red brick contrasts a cheerful yellow door—a surprise coming from Corbin. But I suppose being a bachelor doesn't preclude good design taste.

I'm still floating in a state of shock at today's events and what's going to happen next. Or what I hope happens next. Hearing that Corbin used to be a bullied kid instead of the popular jock I assumed filled in some of the questions I had about him. And endeared him to me even more.

Slamming the car door behind me, I meet Corbin behind his truck, and we walk up to his front porch. "You have a lovely home; pretty big for a single guy, though."

"I thought I'd be optimistic about potentially filling the space with a family." The soft admission melts me and an odd combination of desire and compassion swirls in my stomach.

"How big are you talking?" I tease as we step inside the open concept first floor with a staircase going up the left wall.

"Well, I've got four rooms. One's the master, the other's my home office. That leaves two to start." He faces me with a question in his expression like he's waiting for me to call it quits.

Which I should if we're already talking kids. But I meant what I said earlier. I'm with Corbin—for better or worse.

"Good to know." I walk the length of the living room, bypassing a large cream-colored sectional, and notice the lack of photos on the walls. It's the only noticeable absence in an otherwise cozy home. "Where are all of your pictures?"

He rubs a hand down his shadowed cheek and sighs. "I'm not much of a picture-taking guy. Old habits die hard."

His implication is clear. Photos aren't my favorite thing either; all I can ever seem to see are my flaws.

"I understand. Everything else is still beautiful. Did you hire someone?"

"Do you really want to know? Because I can think of a few things we could do instead, and they'd be a hell of a lot more interesting."

Excitement skitters down my spine along with a healthy dose of nerves. This isn't my typical behavior—sleeping with a man on the first date. *Your only date.* But I knew where we were headed the moment I suggested going back to his place, and the anticipation of what's to come heats my blood.

I reach a hand out for Corbin to take, his larger hand warm and calloused. "You have a point. Why don't you show me your room?"

He grins and leads me upstairs to the master where a huge king-sized bed dominates the room. Once again, the walls remain empty of frames, but my focus isn't on decor anymore.

"So, what happens now?" I ask awkwardly as we stand in silence waiting for the other to make a move.

"Now, I kiss you." He tugs me into his embrace and our lips meet again. This kiss is different from the earlier ones, though.

Those were tentative, searching, but we're past that point after he ate me out in the nosebleeds. It's burned away the majority of our hesitancy to leave behind a passionate fury to be nearer, bare skin sliding against the other.

My mouth opens eagerly to his, and we stumble backwards until I hit the end of his mattress. Corbin's hands skim up my thighs then higher, taking my dress with him until I'm left standing in my pink cotton underwear and lace bra. The air conditioning hums above us blasting cold air over my exposed skin, and I resist the urge to cover up—as much for warmth as the sudden, nagging fear that he won't like what he sees.

"Damn, you're beautiful—all sexy curves waiting for me to explore." The tone of awe coming from Corbin eases me a bit; I don't think he's lying, but like he said earlier, old habits die hard.

Ignoring his comment, I pull at his navy henley. "And what about you?"

He bends for me to remove the shirt over his head, and I'm left staring at a tan muscular chest that leads to a vee of ridged muscles. My tongue feels swollen in my mouth as I'm left speechless and anxious to feel him underneath me. An unbidden image of a fantasy I had years ago pops up. Me riding a man's six-pack, sliding hot and wet over those hard muscles until he takes my thighs in a bruising grip and yanks me to his mouth.

A gush of wetness soaks my panties as I replace the imaginary man with Corbin, eyeing his beard and wanting to feel that scratch between my legs again.

"See something you like, baby? Because I know I do," Corbin teases. Slowly, I lower myself to the bed and crawl back until my head rests on his pillow, allowing my legs to splay open in the most brazen act I've done in my life. *Second, if we're counting letting a man go down on me in a public stadium.*

"Then what are you waiting for? I'm yours for the taking."

With a growl, he tears at the rest of his clothes until he stands naked and proud—his erection bobbing against his stomach, thick and hard. My pussy clenches at the sight, and I'm grateful that I've been using toys all these years to get off. I may be a technical virgin—never having actually slept with anyone—but I've got a cache of dildos, vibrators, and more stashed away at home.

"Are you? That's really good to hear." Corbin moves to hover over me as he rests on his elbows before allowing the weight of his body to sink into mine, and the weight is a welcome sensation. Nuzzling my ear, he whispers, "Are you ready for me to fuck you, Darcy baby? To lick and suck your pretty nipples? To ride you so hard you're begging me to let you come?"

The dirty words make me ache, and I can only moan in response. I want all of those things and more. "Yes, please...Please, Corbin, I need it, need you..."

A rumble of pleasure vibrates from his chest, and he shifts lower. Burrowing a hand beneath my back, I feel the claps on my bra unsnap and the scrap of lace falls away. His bearded cheek scrapes against a nipple before heat engulfs it as his mouth tugs on the sensitive tip. My back arches at the new attention.

Frantic hands tunnel into his hair as I hold him to me, urging him to continue. "Don't stop."

Corbin releases the reddened tip with a pop and tilts his head. "But what about this?" He circles my other nipple with his tongue. "Your breasts deserve equal attention, so ripe and full. Don't you agree, baby?"

He doesn't wait for an answer, just lowers his head again to nip at the engorged bud. A mew of surprise leaves me at the unexpected bite, but he soothes the slight sting with the flat of his tongue.

When I'd touched myself before, it'd been nice, but I assumed my breasts weren't that sensitive. How wrong I was. Clearly, I needed Corbin to show me my error.

And I want him to show me a lot more.

CHAPTER TWELVE

CORBIN

Darcy's body undulates under me as I alternate between licking and sucking her nipples. Their color keeps deepening—blush pink to deep red—and I wonder if I can get her off just by playing her breasts.

But I want to taste her again too much to try now. Not to mention my dick. It's leaking like a sieve, pre-cum seeping from the tip. All these years of abstinence; I'm ready to end it tonight.

I track kisses down her round stomach to the curls protecting her sex. "So soft, baby. Soft like silk and so warm." I murmur the words almost unconsciously as I part her thighs wider to see her glossy pussy. "So wet for me. Aren't you?"

She lifts her hips in supplication. "Please, Corbin... I need you."

Unwilling to deny her anything, I bury my face between her thighs and mimic the moves I learned she enjoyed earlier. It doesn't take long before she's coming on my tongue, and I rise up to fit my dick against her clenching opening.

"Tell me you want this, Darcy. One last time to back out because once we cross this line, I'm not letting you go."

"I want this. I want you. I don't want to go back." Her serious eyes meet mine, and the moment transcends pure lust. This is more than physical attraction; however crazy it may seem, there are real feelings between us.

Holding her gaze, I slowly push forward, and wet warmth surrounds me. My lungs struggle to drag in air at the tight fit like nothing I've ever felt before.

"Fuck...Baby, you feel so good." I groan as her legs wrap around my waist, her heels digging into my back, and I slide deeper. Darcy moans in response, setting off a need in me to hear more of her breathy sounds of pleasure.

Seated to the hilt, I begin a pumping rhythm until I'm slamming into her so hard the headboard slaps against the wall. Maybe I should've started out slow and easy, but I can't resist fucking her hard and fast. The drag of my cock through her clasping sheathe shoots sparks throughout my body, and to my embarrassment, I realize I'm not going to last long on this first go. Reaching down, I circle her clit with my thumb to ensure she at least comes with me—her dissatisfaction is not an option.

"Corbin..." Her nails dig into my shoulders, and she cries out as her pussy spasms around me pushing me over the edge with her. Jets of my seed overflow between us creating a sticky, sucking sound as my hips jerk at my orgasm. Collapsing to the side of the bed, I try to catch my breath, my heart racing.

"Are you okay?" I force the question out after managing to wrap an arm around her waist to hold her close.

"Mmm...perfect." Darcy's head turns to face me, and a sleepy, satisfied smile forms on her face. I never want to see it leave, always wanting her to feel this way.

"I didn't hurt you?"

"What? No, of course not," she says vehemently. "It was wonderful. You were wonderful."

I sigh in relief. "I'm glad...It was my first time, as humiliating as it is to admit."

Her eyes widen in shock. "Are you serious?"

Nodding, I caress her arm. "It took a long time for me to become comfortable in my body after losing the weight. And then, the only women who showed interest were obvious only after what I could give them financially. It was just easier with everything I was building to stay single and celibate."

"That makes sense, although I'm still surprised. I suppose I should tell you this was my first time, too." A twinkle appears in her blue eyes. "Now, we're no longer virgins."

"Thank God!" I laugh in agreement before sobering. "It was worth the wait, though, right?"

"Oh, definitely. You're way better than my vibrator." A hand snaps to her mouth as she gasps. I guess she wasn't planning on revealing that interesting bit of information. "I can't believe I told that."

"I'm glad you did. It means we'll be having a lot of fun in the future."

"You don't mind?"

"Why would I? Anything to satisfy my woman. I'm not opposed to a little help in that department."

"Corbin, you are a literal unicorn. I'm not sure many men feel that way."

I lift one shoulder in indifference. "Doesn't matter what they feel anyway."

"No, I guess not." We lay there quietly as the room darkens, the sun setting and leaving shadows behind. "So, what happens now? Are we dating? That seems so trivial compared to today."

"I wasn't kidding when I said I'm in this. You're mine, Darcy." I take a leap of faith and voice what I truly want. "I'd like you to move in with me. Marry me. It's fast, I know. But another week, month, or year isn't going to change how I feel."

"How can you be sure?" Doubt laces her tone, and I understand her fear. But I'm not going to let us stop from having the happy future I know we can build.

"I can't. All I know is I'm falling for you and never want to be apart from you. What do you say?"

"Yes. Like a dumb Disney princess who falls in love at first sight, I'm saying yes." She chuckles before rolling over to rest more fully on my chest. "To all of it. Moving in. Marriage. I've never taken a risk in my life; might as well go all in now and see where it leads me."

"It'll lead you to a life full of ups and downs, but I'll be right beside you—protecting you, loving you as best I can," I promise.

"And I'll do the same."

We seal the vows with a kiss, and like a team winning the World Series, I want to pop champagne and celebrate.

I got the girl.

EPILOGUE ONE

DARCY

ONE YEAR LATER

"One more out, and the Eagles will be heading to the National League Division Championship." The announcer reminds the crowd of the stakes as the pitcher winds up for the pitch. I squeeze Corbin's hand as we sit in the same row where we met a year ago.

So much has changed since then I can hardly fathom it. After giving Bethany notice and paying for a month's rent to give her time to find another roommate, Corbin helped me move my things into his home. She didn't take it well that I was leaving especially with a man she assumed would prefer her over me. And in the end, the tenuous friendship ended.

It was for the best, though. Besides being surrounded by Corbin's love, I realized how often Bethany made comments about my weight or appearance. Little things I'd brushed off at the time, but with distance, it turned out they left more of an impact that I thought.

Free from the sly remarks, Corbin's words of encouragement and love filled the void. We married at the courthouse a week after I moved in. My friends back home tried warning me along with my parents, but I knew it was the right decision for me.

And all these months later, it still proved true.

The fans shouted as the third strike was called, and the Eagles won. Turning to Corbin to hug him, I say, "Congratulations! You deserve this win!"

His goal for the teams had always been to get to the playoffs, and he'd done it. Pride swelled in my chest at all of his hard work paying off.

"I can't believe it's really happening. I've got to talk to Coach; congratulate the team..." He trails off as his gaze surveys the stadium before landing on me again. "We did it."

"You did it. You've earned everything that's coming." I lean up to kiss him, and a burst of love pounds in my chest. I love Corbin—no ifs, ands, or buts. No matter our unconventional start, knowing what I do now, I wouldn't have it any other way.

EPILOGUE TWO

CORBIN
FIVE YEARS LATER

Children's screams bellow from the backyard where the team and their families hang out for tonight's barbeque. It's the All-Star break, and we're celebrating a little downtime before the baseball season starts back up.

Arms wrap around my back to settle on my stomach. "What are you thinking?" Darcy asks as her head rests against my back.

"Just how grateful I am for this break." I turn around and kiss her forehead. "And how happy I am with this life we've built. We did good, huh?"

"Yeah, we did good." She smiles and pecks my cheek. "Who'd have thought?"

Everyone thought we were crazy moving so fast, but we were shattering all of their doubts. Five years and two kids later, I loved my wife and family more every day.

"Despite those assholes from that night, I'm happy as hell that you attended the game that night. I love you, you know?"

"How can I forget? You show me every day. In the way you care for Trevor and Noah. The way you make sure we never want for anything." She tightens her arms around me. "I'm not sure how I got so lucky."

"Let's not start that again," I joke. Every once in a while, old fears crop up, but we deal with them. I remind her that she's beautiful and sexy, and she reminds me that I'm worth loving.

"You're right. Tonight's a night of relaxation and fun."

"And later tonight, it'll be for..." I whisper in her ear in case there's any errant children sneaking around. "Me fucking your tight pussy with my tongue before burying my cock deep inside you. Over and over again until you're too sore to walk tomorrow."

"Corbin," she groans. "You can't say stuff like that when we've got company."

"Why? It's my home, and you're my wife. It's perfectly acceptable to let my wife know to prepare herself for a night loving by her man."

The door leading in from the porch opens as someone steps inside, and we separate with a heated look.

Tonight, I'll be loving Darcy all night. My sexy, curvy wife—the mother of my children and the love of my life.

Ready for more curvy girls to find love?

Check out the first book in the Tees & Jeans series!
The Brother Bias (Book #1)

From the moment Ella Johnson met Gavin Cross, she knew it was love. Older, sexy, and a popular jock, everything about him gets her hot and bothered. There's only one problem...

Gavin's her brother's best friend and doesn't notice her—the curvy nerd crushing on him.

But now Ella's all grown up and unexpectedly stuck living with him for the next week. Can she gather enough courage to finally make a move or will fear stop her from getting the man she's always wanted?

This brother's best friend doesn't know what hits him when the shy girl he knew transforms into a curvy bombshell with a few naughty secrets. Get ready for steamy nights where the line between desire and loyalty blur in a story of second chances!

THANKS FOR READING & DON'T FORGET TO RATE/ REVIEW!

Please consider leaving a rating/review on Amazon, Goodreads, Instagram, TikTok, and/or any other sites you review on.
Ratings & reviews are the #1 way to support an indie author like me.
They don't have to be long or even positive (though I hope you enjoyed this book!). All the algorithms care about are QUANTITY.
The more reviews, the more my books are shown to other potential readers!
And they serve as guides to readers on whether or not to take a chance on an indie author.
I appreciate your support!
XO, Hallie

ABOUT THE AUTHOR

Hallie prefers steamy, insta-love stories where curvy girls are claimed by filthy-talking heroes. And when she ran out of reading material, she decided to write her own stories. If you want a quick, hot read, she's your girl!

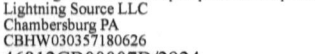